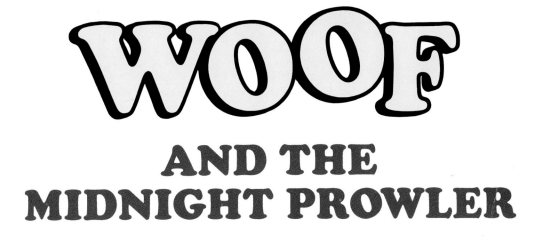

# WOOF
## AND THE
## MIDNIGHT PROWLER

by Danae Dobson
Illustrated by Dee deRosa

WORD PUBLISHING
Dallas · London · Sydney · Singapore

For my two wonderful grandparents, Joe and Alma Kubishta.
You created many special childhood memories for me.
Thank you for the homemade meals,
trips to amusement parks,
and years of laughter and fun.
I love you (even if you don't like dogs very much).

**Woof and the Midnight Prowler**

Copyright ©1989 by Danae Dobson for the text. Copyright ©1989 by Dee deRosa for the illustrations.
All rights reserved. No portion of this book may be reproduced in any form without the written permission
of the publishers, except for brief quotations in reviews.
Library of Congress Cataloging-in-Publication Data
Dobson, Danae.
Woof and the midnight prowler / by Danae Dobson: illustrated by Dee deRosa.
  p. cm.
Summary: When the Petersons go to visit Grandma's farm, she is not impressed by their unattractive dog
Woof, but he redeems himself in her eyes by an act of bravery.
  ISBN 0-8499-8347-9:
  [1. Dogs — Fiction. 2. Grandmothers — Fiction. 3. Farm life — Fiction.] I. DeRosa, Dee, ill. II. Title.
PZ7.D6614Wq 1989
[E] — dc20                                                                                      89-16622
Printed in the United States of America                                                              CIP
9801239RA987654321                                                                                    AC

# A MESSAGE FROM
# Dr. James Dobson

Before you read about this dog named Woof perhaps you would like to know how these books came to be written. When my children, Danae and Ryan, were young, I often told them stories at bedtime. Many of those tales were about pet animals who were loved by people like those in our own family. Later, I created more stories while driving the children to school in our car pool. The kids began to fall in love with these pets, even though they existed only in our minds. I found out just how much they loved these animals when I made the mistake of telling them a story in which one of their favorite pets died. There were so many tears I had to bring him back to life!

These tales made a special impression on Danae. At the age of twelve, she decided to write her own book about her favorite animal, Woof, and see if Word Publishers would like to print it. She did, and they did, and in the process she became the youngest author in Word's history. Now, ten years later, Danae has written five more, totally new adventures with Woof and the Petersons. And she is still Word's youngest author!

Danae has discovered a talent God has given her, and it all started with our family spending time together, talking about a dog and the two children who loved him. We hope that not only will you enjoy Woof's adventures but that you and your family will enjoy the time spent reading them together. Perhaps you also will discover a talent God has given you.

The morning sun shone brightly through Mark Peterson's bedroom window. "Wake up, Krissy!" Mark called to his sister across the hall. "We don't want to be late to Grandma's today."

Grandma Peterson had one of the best farms in Idaho. It was filled with all sorts of interesting animals, fruit trees and farm equipment. Mark loved to ride the tractors, and Krissy enjoyed helping her grandmother make goodies. They always had fun at her farm.

After breakfast the family piled into the station wagon, and Father began backing the car down the winding driveway.

"Wait!" Mark cried, glancing about him. "Where's Woof?"

As if responding to the question, a shaggy mutt with a crooked leg and a sorrowful appearance sped across the front yard and bounded into the back of the station wagon, knocking over several suitcases.

Krissy patted the dog on the head. "Sorry, Woof. We just couldn't forget to take you on this trip."

Woof licked her face.

On the way to the farm, Father suggested that the family enjoy devotions and prayer. It was common for the Petersons to read the Bible and pray on long car trips. Mrs. Peterson read first, and then Mark and Krissy turned to the story of Joseph and his coat of many colors. They loved that story because Joseph never got discouraged even though everything seemed to go wrong for him. When they were finished, Father led the family in prayer. He asked God to be with them on the way to the farm and to keep them safe from any danger. The Petersons' faith was very important to their family.

After devotions the children read books and magazines to keep themselves busy, but it wasn't long before they got tired of sitting in the crowded car.

"I'm thirsty!" Mark complained.

"Me too, and I have to go to the bathroom," Krissy added.

"Now, children, be patient. I'm sure there will be a gas station up the road," Mrs. Peterson said.

Even Woof seemed uncomfortable as he sat panting in the back seat of the car.

Before long, the Peterson car pulled into a service station at the side of the country road. Father put gas in the tank while the children played with Woof around the small building. No one noticed the pickup truck that pulled up beside them. A large man got out of the truck and went inside the station. In the back of the truck were twin boys who looked like pure trouble. Their hair was uncombed, and their faces looked grubby from not having soap and water on them for many days. Mark and Krissy didn't pay much attention to them, although they wondered why the boys kept looking at them suspiciously and whispering.

Then it happened. Just as Woof was running to catch a stick Mark had thrown, one of the boys threw a rock from the back of the truck. It hit the dog in the shoulder with a thud. Woof let out a yelp and rolled end over end. Mark and Krissy gasped as they ran over to their injured dog and bent over him. In the background they could hear the two boys laughing wildly.

As soon as Krissy saw that Woof was all right, she marched over to her father to tell him what had happened. But before she could begin to explain, the man started the truck and drove out of the gas station.

"Oh, no!" Krissy cried.

"What happened?" Father asked, seeing the tears in his daughter's eyes.

After Krissy told what the two boys had done, Mr. Peterson became very upset. "I can't believe anyone would do something so cruel to an innocent animal." Then he walked over to Woof and checked for broken bones. After finding none, he cleaned the blood off the dog's fur and gave him some fresh water to drink. Woof didn't appear to be in great pain, but Mark could tell that the experience had made him very sad.

Even Jake, the gas station attendant, noticed the sadness in Woof's eyes as he patted the scraggly head. "That was a rotten thing to do," he said. "Them Harper boys is always causin' trouble around here. Someone needs to take a stick to their backsides."

In a short while Woof appeared to be feeling better. So the family climbed into the car again and said good-bye to Jake. The rest of the ride was long and hot, with temperatures rising into the eighties. Three hours later the family finally reached the dirt road that led to Grandma Peterson's.

"We're almost there, kids," Mother said. "Get your belongings together."

Up ahead they could see an older woman waving to them excitedly.
"There's Grandma!" Krissy shouted.

They forgot all about the long ride as they tumbled out of the car and ran to greet her. Even with a sore shoulder, Woof was close at their heels, while Mr. and Mrs. Peterson followed at a slower pace. Adults don't like to run very much, as we all know.

"Oh! It's so good to see you," Grandma said warmly as she hugged the children.

"It has been a long time since we were here last, Grandma," said Mark. "Hey! I don't think you've ever met our great dog, Woof!"

He bent over to give his pet a hug while Grandma scratched her head and wrinkled her brow. "Is this what all the commotion has been about lately?" she asked. "He certainly isn't a pretty sight! Look at that crooked leg! And those floppy ears!"

"Well, remember, Mom," Father added. "He did save your grandson's life."

Grandma smiled at Mark as she remembered how Woof had kept him from being hit by a car not long ago.

"Well, I don't see how a dog that ugly can be worth a whole lot, but he's welcome anyway," she laughed. "Come on inside. I've got dinner waiting."

While the family visited with Grandma, Woof began to explore the area. Since the farm was miles from the nearest town, there were many strange animals he had never seen before. Woof was fascinated by the cows, pigs and chickens. The chickens were not so thrilled to see Woof, of course. They reacted to his playfulness by cackling wildly and scurrying to stay out of his way. But Woof continued to chase them around the coop and nip at their

feathers in a playful fashion. After a while he left the chickens and went on
to explore the other sights and smells of the farm.

Out in the meadow he could see fields of wheat blowing gently in the
breeze and a tiny stream running through the center of the farm. Woof
completely forgot about his sore shoulder as he explored the pastures, chasing
rabbits and running through the thick grass. This was the most fun he had
had in a long time!

He barely noticed that it was getting dark as he continued to explore the barns, run in the fields and sniff the unusual smells that were everywhere. In the distance he heard Mark call his name. Maybe he had some table scraps to offer. Woof began trotting back to the farmhouse, exhausted from the heat and the fun of his adventurous afternoon.

Mark met him at the door. "Woof! Where have you been all this time?" Woof licked his hand happily.

"Grandma says you will have to sleep out there on the porch tonight, but you'll be okay. I made you a soft bed and gave you some food." Woof loved to eat more than anything in the world.

Just then, Krissy unlatched the screen door. "Mark, do you think it's safe out here for Woof?"

Mark looked unsure. "I think so," he replied. "Grandma said he'd be all right."

With that, the children gave their dog a pat and hurried off to bed. Woof circled his blanket three times, as dogs have done for thousands of years. He then curled up in a little ball. But Woof couldn't sleep. Hours passed and yet he lay still, listening to the crickets and an occasional hoot from an owl. Finally, drowsiness began to overtake him and slowly he drifted off to sleep.

No sooner had he closed his eyes than a strange noise came from the chicken coop. Woof jumped up and cocked his ears from side to side, his heart thumping rapidly. Did he just imagine he had heard it? After a few moments, another noise echoed in the night, followed by frantic squawking from the chickens. Woof trotted to the coop, his eyes straining to see in the darkness. He stopped when he got to the door and peered in. A strange scent drifted into his nostrils.

Suddenly in the corner he saw something moving! A mean, doglike creature was stalking in the darkness. He had a few feathers on his nose, and
his ears stood straight up. Woof didn't know that the animal in the shadows
was a coyote, but he understood that it was his enemy. He also knew that
the chickens belonged to the farm and the killer didn't. The coyote wheeled
toward Woof and growled angrily. He crouched low, preparing to fight.

Meanwhile the Petersons had also heard the noise and came outside with a flashlight.

"Woof! Here, boy!" Mark called from the porch. Hearing a human voice, the coyote dashed past Woof in the darkness and made his escape. Woof didn't chase him because Mark had called his name. The Petersons hurried to the coop and turned on the light. There stood Woof surrounded by at least a million feathers, but the frightened chickens had managed to escape and were perched around the top of the coop.

"I knew it!" Grandma wailed. "That no–good dog has gotten into my best chickens!"

Mark ran over and stared at the mess. "Woof! Why did you do it?" he asked ashamedly.

"I can't believe it," said Father. "He's never tried to hurt anything before. I am very disappointed. Let's tie him up for tonight and decide what to do in the morning."

Mother nodded in agreement. Krissy and Mark looked at each other sadly. They knew Woof was in great trouble. Grandma Peterson tried to be nice about the matter, but she was very angry at the ugly dog.

"Poor Woof," Krissy sighed. "Everything has gone wrong for him today."

For the rest of the night and the next day, Woof was kept tied to a fence post by a short rope. He was very unhappy. He wanted to trot around the yard and explore the barns. He had never been tied up before and didn't like the feeling. In fact, the rope got tangled around a bush and kept him tightly controlled. He could hardly move.

About midmorning, Krissy left with her mother and grandmother to pick berries in the meadow. Woof wanted to go with them and barked twice as they walked down the path, but they just told him to hush.

Then Mark passed by on his way to the barn with two workmen. Woof barked again, but they didn't hear him.

All day long he watched the children as they walked in the fields and rode tractors and ran and played. Oh, how he wanted to be out there with them! Woof knew the family was upset with him over something — especially Grandma. Every time she passed him she shook her finger and called him a "naughty dog!" It was a long, miserable day for Woof.

By the time evening came, everyone was tired and hungry. Woof watched as the family passed by him on the way to the house. No one noticed him at all as he sat whimpering by the fence post. After dinner Mrs. Peterson went outside to take Woof a bone and bring him some fresh water. His sad eyes made her feel sorry for him as she set down his water dish.

"We're going home tomorrow, boy," she said softly.

Woof wagged his tail and looked up at her hopefully. Mrs. Peterson petted him for a few minutes and then made her way back to the house.

That night Woof stood and waited patiently for the children to come outside and say good-night to him as they always did. But this night they
didn't come. Darkness fell on the countryside, and the minutes turned into
hours, but still no one came to see him. Finally he gave up and lay down on
the cool grass by the fence. It began to get very late, but again, Woof could
not sleep. He knew the strange doglike creature might return, only this
time he was tied with a rope. What could he do? He kept his eyes fixed on
the chicken coop and listened closely. The later it got, the more nervous Woof
became. After a while he could no longer stay in one place. Anxiously he
paced back and forth by the fence, staring into the blackened night.

Sometime after midnight a dark shadow moved near the coop. The prowler had returned! Woof's body tensed, and he leaned against the rope that held him captive. The shadow slipped to the door of the coop. Woof couldn't stand it. He heaved violently against the rope and growled threateningly. Suddenly, the rope broke and set him free.

Chickens in the coop were squawking and frantically flapping their wings. Woof raced toward the coop with all the energy he had. This time he didn't pause when he reached the door. The surprised coyote had no time to prepare before Woof was on him. There in the night the two animals began a fight to the death. Growling, biting and tumbling through the darkness, Woof gave everything he had to the struggle.

The chickens scattered in terror, and a horse in a nearby barn neighed. Every animal on the farm knew a battle was underway. Fortunately so did the Petersons. The entire family seemed to run from the farm house at the same time. Even Grandma came running down the front porch with her robe flying in the night air.

As Woof and the coyote fought, they knocked over a stack of empty feed barrels that stood by the door. The coyote was then trapped inside. When he heard human voices, he stopped fighting and backed into a corner of the coop. Woof, breathing heavily, stood guard with his head low. The coyote had had enough. He had never tangled with a fighter like this dumb-looking dog! He wanted no more battle!

The Petersons reached the coop and directed a flashlight over the barrels and inside the small building. Spotting Woof and the coyote, Grandma gasped in shock. "Oh, my!" she said. "I'd better get a rope."

With that, she headed back toward the house. The rest of the family stayed outside and kept watch to make sure the coyote didn't get away. Mark and Krissy were happy that Woof was not responsible for the chickens that were terrified the night before.

When Grandma returned with the rope, Father managed to toss it around the coyote's neck and tie him in the barn. It was a very exciting night for the entire Peterson family! As they made their way back to the house, Mark suddenly remembered that they had not seen Woof since he trapped the coyote.

"Where's Woof?" he asked. "Is he hurt?"

They found Woof sitting on the front porch in the dark, licking his wounds. Mark hugged the dog affectionately and untied the length of rope that still hung around his neck. "Woof, you're the best dog anyone ever had!" he said happily.

Even Grandma was pleased with the heroic dog. "I'm sorry I scolded you for something you didn't do," she apologized, patting him on the head. "I'm going to give you some nice, juicy steak bones!"

Woof panted happily and wagged his tail. He wasn't certain what Grandma had just offered him, but her voice sounded kind.

"I sure am glad Woof wasn't the one that upset those chickens," Father said. "I was afraid we could never have turned him loose again, even at home."

Woof was brought into the farmhouse and his wounds were cleaned and disinfected. Then he was fed and given a warm bed — in the house this time. He was very happy to be loved by the family again.

"Well, let's get some sleep," Father said, yawning. "We've had enough excitement for one night."

The next morning Mr. Peterson called the Department of Fish and Game and asked if they would come and pick up the coyote. They said they would be there at noon to take him far away. Then they would let him go. In the meantime the Petersons sat down to a wonderful breakfast of biscuits, bacon, orange juice and cereal. Cooking great meals was one of Grandma's specialties, and this was one of her best.

After breakfast the children and Woof played out in the field until the men from the Department of Fish and Game arrived. Woof was the first one to greet them as he made a dash toward their truck, barking happily. The family and Woof watched as the men led the coyote from the barn and into the truck. When the coyote saw Woof, he growled angrily.

"It's all right, Woof," Mark said kindly. "There's no way he can cause any more trouble, thanks to you."

When the truck left, Father suggested that they pack the car and prepare to leave for home.

After everything was taken care of, Grandma came outside to tell them good-bye. "Thanks for coming to visit, and please come again soon," she said, hugging the children. "And don't forget to bring Woof; he's the bravest and smartest dog I've ever seen. I'd love to have him around the farm all the time."

As if understanding her kind words, Woof licked her hand.

"That's our hero!" Mark added, giving Woof a hug.

After everyone had said good-bye four or five more times, Grandma stood watching as the car made its way down the dirt road and toward the main highway. In the distance she could see a small animal poke his furry head out of the rear window and look back at her. His strange ears wiggled in the breeze.

"That dumb-looking dog really is special," she said to herself. "I'll miss him."

Several hours later the Petersons stopped at Jake's service station again to fill up their car with gas. As they drove into the driveway, they couldn't believe their eyes. At the vending machine stood the Harper twins! They were busy buying soft drinks and didn't see the Petersons' station wagon roll to a stop.

Father opened the door and intended to talk to the boys, but Woof had a better idea. He jumped out of the car and headed for the twins.

As the boys were putting coins into the machine, Woof ran up behind them and let out his loudest, deepest, meanest bark. The twins jumped at least two feet in the air and screamed in terror. They turned and ran to their truck as fast as they could, with Woof nipping at their bare feet.

Krissy and Mark looked at each other and burst out laughing. Even Mr. and Mrs. Peterson had a hard time hiding their smiles. And would you believe — even Woof had a smile on his doggy face, too.